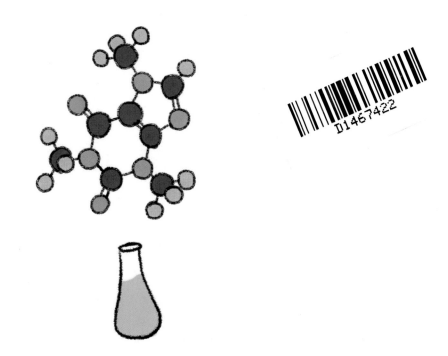

This book is dedicated to all of the mothers raising the next generation of scientists.

Lab Coat

Long Pants

Safety first!
When we first get to the lab,

3

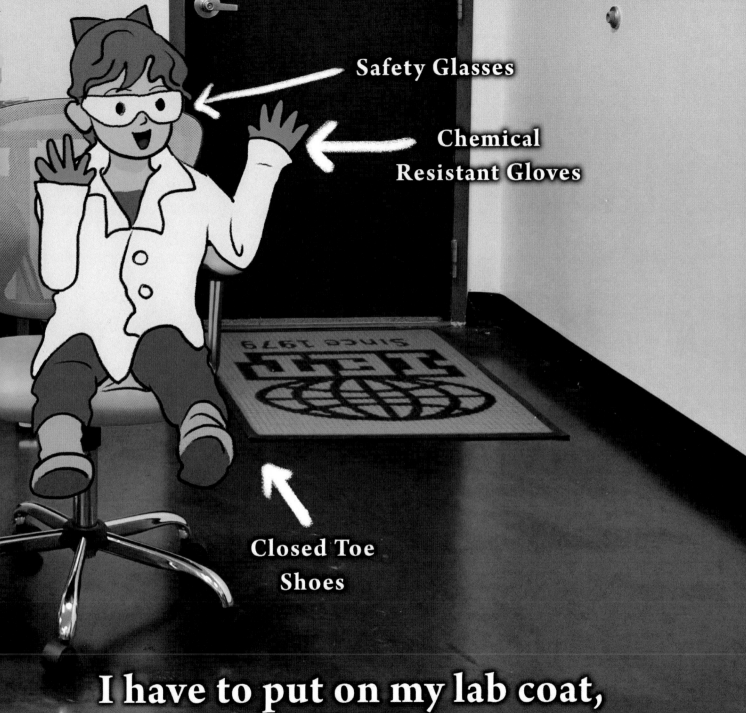

Safety Glasses

Chemical Resistant Gloves

Closed Toe Shoes

I have to put on my lab coat, gloves and safety glasses.

4

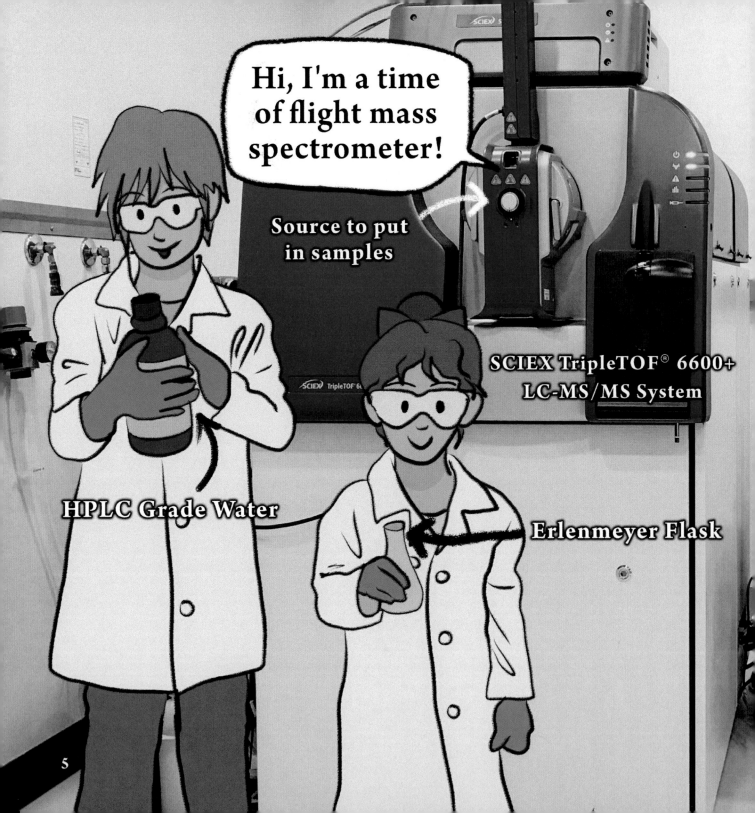

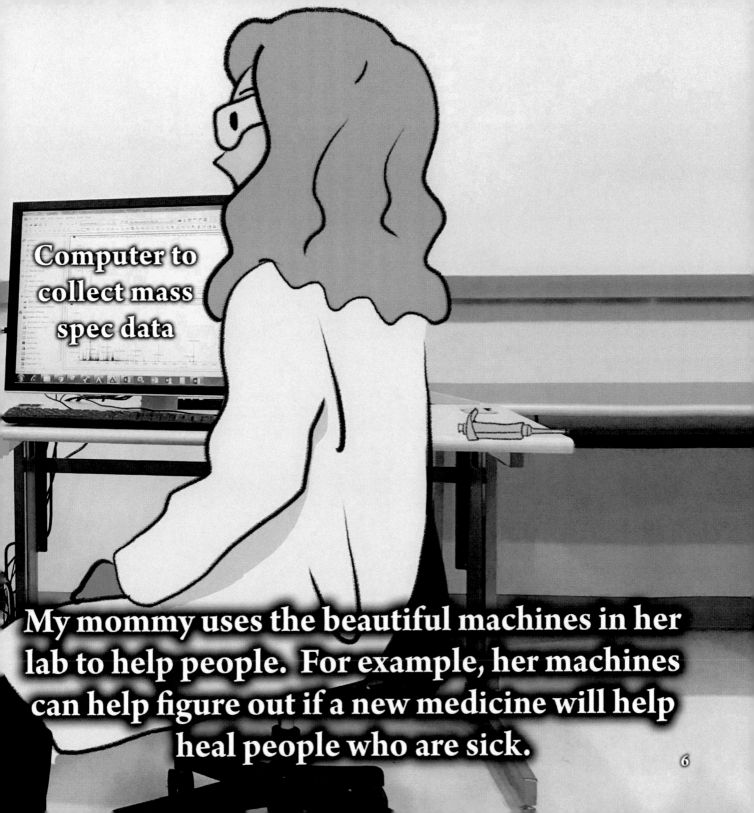

Computer to collect mass spec data

My mommy uses the beautiful machines in her lab to help people. For example, her machines can help figure out if a new medicine will help heal people who are sick.

The machine she uses is called a mass spectrometer. A mass spectrometer can weigh things kind of like a big scale,

Thermo Orbitrap
Fusion Lumos

Hi, I'm an
Orbitrap mass
spectrometer!

similar to the one that the doctor uses
to weigh you. This scale measures tiny things
that we can't see with our eyes.

The things that my mommy is looking at are so small that you cannot see them even with a microsope.

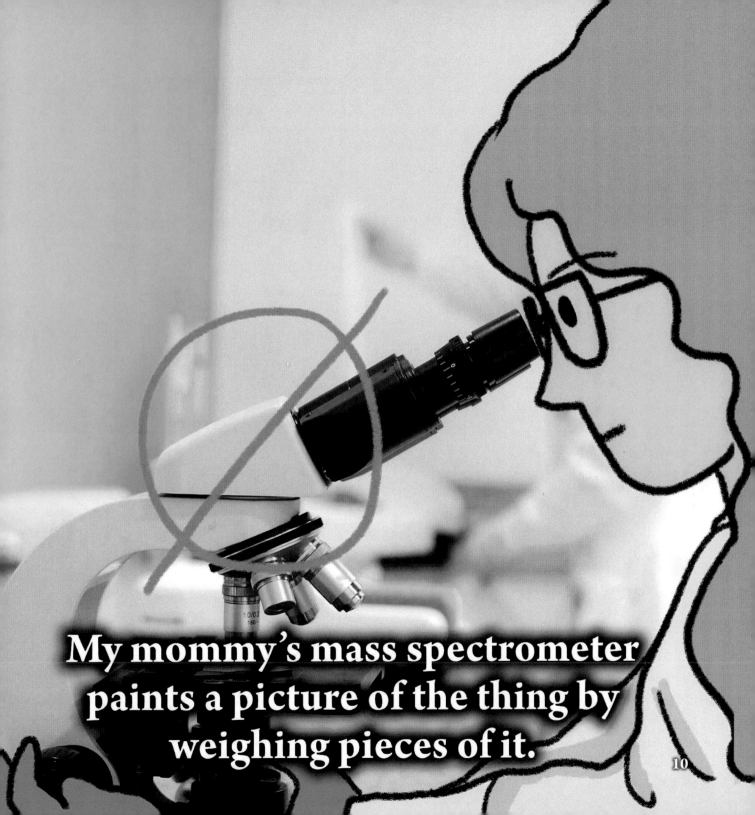

My mommy's mass spectrometer paints a picture of the thing by weighing pieces of it.

10

There are molecules here too!

Everything around us is made up of tiny bundles of spheres that we can't see. Everything including you, your teddy bear, and the water in your glass.

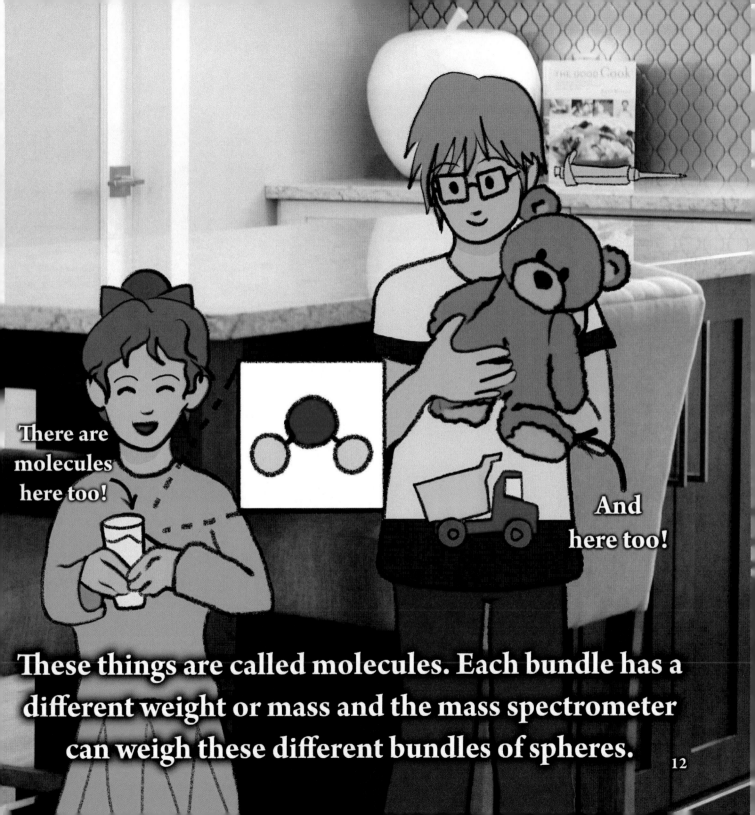

There are molecules here too!

And here too!

These things are called molecules. Each bundle has a different weight or mass and the mass spectrometer can weigh these different bundles of spheres.

12

This is how my mommy explains the tiny bundles of spheres or molecules. There are two identical boxes. These are the molecules. Inside one box is a balloon. Inside the other box is a watermelon.

Because the boxes are so teeny tiny, you can't see inside the boxes. These boxes make up everything around you. To understand more about these molecules, the mass spectrometer can weigh them.

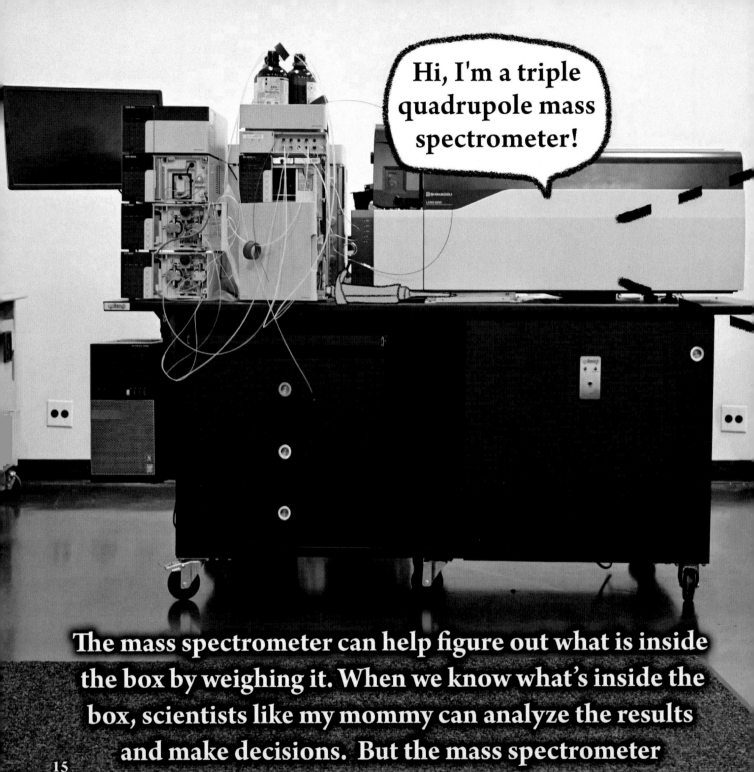

The mass spectrometer can help figure out what is inside the box by weighing it. When we know what's inside the box, scientists like my mommy can analyze the results and make decisions. But the mass spectrometer

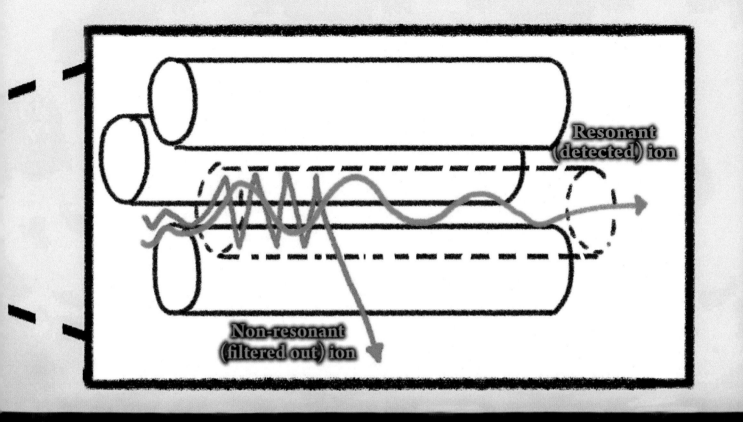

Resonant (detected) ion

Non-resonant (filtered out) ion

doesn't look like a scale. How does it weigh the molecules? Inside the mass spectrometer, there is a sorting machine, which has an electric field around it. Only molecules with a certain weight will reach the detector.

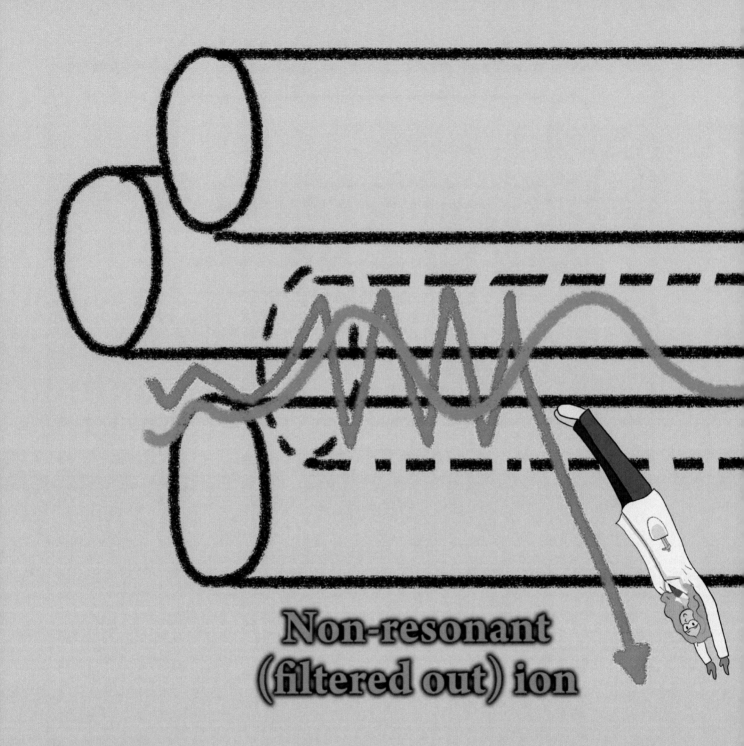

Non-resonant
(filtered out) ion

Resonant
(detected) ion

We are too large, but it's still fun
to imagine flying through
the mass spectrometer.

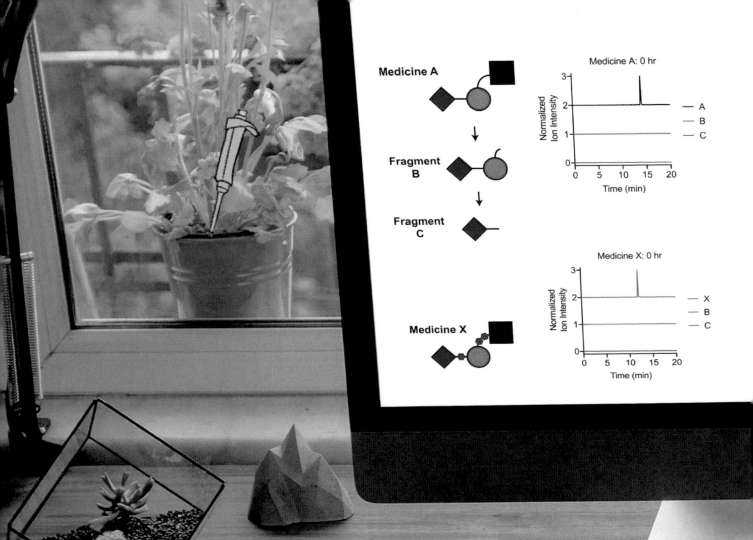

My mommy uses the mass spectrometer to investigate new medicines for a type of illness called lung cancer. She has been working with a team of scientist friends to see how well this new medicine will work inside the body. First the scientist friends tried Medicine A, but it wasn't very good. Medicine A fell apart

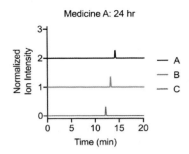

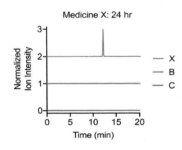

very quickly during treatment. My mommy could detect pieces of the medicine with the mass spectrometer. After more experiments, the scientist friends found that Medicine X was a lot better. The experiment results showed that Medicine X was more stable and a better medicine to help treat sick people.

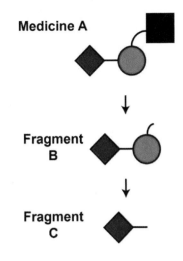
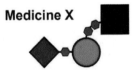

Sometimes my mommy goes to mass spectrometry meetings to share ideas with other scientists.

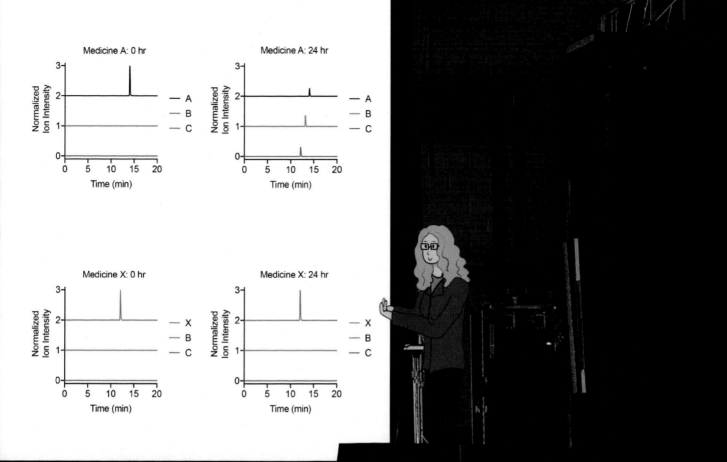

I miss her a lot when she is gone, but she always brings me back cool science toys. 🐸

My mommy is a super scientist.

When I grow up, I want to be a mass spectrometry scientist too.

Acknowledgements

The inspiration for this book was my son's curiosity in all of the "beautiful machines" at my office. It started with a discussion and some crude drawings and grew into this little book project.

Thank you to my sisters for their support. Thank you to Ela for the illustrations and putting up with my changes. Thank you to Eda for the photography and editing help.

Thank you to (almost Dr.) Jeff Montgomery for his official science guidance.

Thank you to IET, International Equipment Trading, for allowing the photography of some of the laboratory equipment featured in the book.

Special thanks to Shimadzu, Thermo, Sciex, and ASMS for the prompt approvals of the use of some of the images featured in the book.

Made in the USA
Las Vegas, NV
17 May 2022